...... ball. A hard kick. It ...... like a cannonball towards the kitchen window. Cripes! Jim was just wondering how many weeks' pocket money it would take to pay for a new window when something amazing happened. From nowhere, a tabby streak flashed into view, and two outstretched paws deflected the ball harmlessly into a bush.

Read all about Sammy, the amazing footballing cat, in this fast-paced, funny Young Corgi – perfect for building reading confidence.

YOUNG CORGI BOOKS

Young Corgi books are perfect when you are looking for great books to read on your own. They are full of exciting stories and entertaining pictures and can be tackled with confidence. There are funny books, scary books, spine-tingling stories and mysterious ones. Whatever your interests you'll find something in Young Corgi to suit you: from ponies to football, from families to ghosts. The books are written by some of the most famous and popular of today's children's authors, and by some of the best new talents, too.

Whether you read one chapter a night, or devour the whole book in one sitting, you'll love Young Corgi books. The more you read, the more you'll want to read!

Other YoungCorgi books to get your teeth into

BLACK QUEEN by Michael Morpurgo

LIZZIE ZIPMOUTH by Jacqueline Wilson

ANIMAL CRACKERS by Narinder Dhami

SAMMY'S SUPER SEASON

For Lily and, of course, Sammy

SAMMY'S SUPER SEASON
A YOUNG CORGI BOOK : 0 552 546615

PRINTING HISTORY
Young Corgi edition published 2000

1 3 5 7 9 10 8 6 4 2

Set in 17/21pt Bembo

Young Corgi Books are published by Transworld Publishers,
61-63 Uxbridge Road, London W5 5SA,
a division of The Random House Group Ltd,
in Australia by Random House Australia (Pty) Ltd,
20 Alfred Street, Milsons Point, Sydney, NSW 2061,
in New Zealand by Random House New Zealand Ltd,
18 Poland Road, Glenfield, Auckland 10,
and in South Africa by Random House (Pty) Ltd,
Endulini, 5a Jubilee Road, Parktown 2193

Printed and bound in Great Britain by
Cox & Wyman Ltd, Reading, Berkshire

Sammy's Super Season

Lindsay Camp

Illustrated by Judy Brown

Books to get your teeth into

YOUNG CORGI

Chapter One

Sammy's First Save

Sammy's favourite thing in all the world was watching football on TV. He'd curl up on the sofa and watch every match he possibly could, even really boring ones between teams with funny foreign names. He was absolutely football crazy.

Nothing very unusual about that,
you're probably thinking. Except that
Sammy's the one on the left. Yes,
that's right, the furry one with the
fishy breath and the sticky-out
whiskers.

The only problem was, Sammy
belonged to Harry – that's him on the
right, the boy-shaped one, with the
hair that needs brushing. And Harry
didn't like football very much at all.
So they were always fighting over
what to watch.

If Harry turned on one of his favourite programmes, like *Space Geeks* or *Cyberwarzone*, when a match was on the other side, Sammy would sit on the sofa and sulk. And once, when Harry reached for the remote control to change channels in the middle of Borussia Munchenbunchen versus Atletico Santiago de Compostella, Sammy scratched his hand so badly he had to go and put on a sticking plaster.

But the rest of the time — whenever there wasn't any football on TV, that is — Sammy and Harry were the best of friends. Sammy slept curled up at the foot of Harry's bed. He sat on Harry's lap and purred while Harry played on the computer. And quite often they even shared a bowl of

SoopaMeggaKrunch with warm milk for their breakfast.

One day, Harry's best friend, Jim, came round after school. It was a sunny day, so they played in the garden. They did all the usual stuff. They made weapons out of sticks. They climbed the tree. And they had a slug race (which, surprisingly, was won by the slug with the arrow pointing at it, in a very exciting finish). Then Jim spotted a ball lying in the flower bed, one that a kind uncle had given Harry for Christmas and which had never been used.

"Let's play football," he said.

"Boring," said Harry. "Let's go and play on the computer." And without even waiting for Jim to answer, he headed indoors.

Jim aimed a kick at the ball. A hard kick. It hurtled like a cannonball towards the kitchen window. Cripes! Jim was just wondering how many weeks' pocket money it would take to pay for a new window when something amazing happened. From nowhere, a tabby streak flashed into view, and two outstretched paws deflected the ball harmlessly into a bush.

"Sammy!" gasped Jim. He could hardly believe his eyes. "You saved me!"

Sammy had settled down on the lawn, and was doing some quite complicated licking underneath his leg, as if nothing had happened. Maybe, thought Jim, just maybe, it had been an accident. Perhaps Sammy had been dashing indoors for his tea, and the ball had just happened to bounce off him? There was only one way to find out. At the other end of the garden, nowhere near any windows, Jim made a goal with his sweatshirt and a large empty flowerpot. He ran up and shot. A tabby blur – another incredi-

ble save! And another, and another. No matter how hard Jim tried, he couldn't score a single goal. He ran inside to find Harry.

"You won't believe this," he panted. "Come in the garden, and see . . ."

Chapter Two

Sammy Goes to School

Jim was right, Harry couldn't believe
it. At first, that is. But after he'd seen
Sammy make a string of astonishing
saves, shot after shot, there was no
getting away from it.

"Sammy's a brilliant goalkeeper!" he
breathed.

"He's absolutely fantastic," gasped
Jim, who was exhausted from trying
to get a shot past him.

Sammy himself had by now trotted
off inside to see if anyone had put
out his tea for him. Harry and Jim
collapsed on the grass, not quite

knowing what to do. "How come we never knew before?" said Jim.

"I suppose he's never had a chance to show us," said Harry. "You know football comes about six zillionth on my list of Favourite Things to Do – just after maths homework."

Jim looked puzzled. "So how's he learned to play, if you didn't teach him?"

"Easy," said Harry. "By watching TV."

After that, Jim came round to play football with Sammy two or three times a week. And even Harry went out and took a few shots from time to time, when he saw Sammy out in the garden, looking hopeful.

Then, one day, Sammy got his first big break. Harry's class was having a Bring Your Pet to School Day. And, of course, Harry wanted to take Sammy. It wasn't easy, though, because after watching football on TV and playing football in the garden, Sammy's favourite thing was eating. And he was getting rather fat – almost too big to fit in the cat basket.

At last, Harry succeeded in cram-ming him in, and they set off. When they arrived at school, Harry took Sammy straight up to the classroom. All kinds of animals were already there: fish, guinea pigs, rabbits, gerbils, a rat and even a chameleon. Chloe Palmer was holding a wriggling ball of fluff. "It's a chinchilla," she said. "D'you want to stroke her?"

"All right," said Harry. And he put Sammy's basket down on Mrs Webb's

Because the basket fell onto the floor with a crash, breaking the catch that held the lid shut and catapulting Sammy out into the classroom.

"Eeeeeeeeeek!" screamed Chloe, eardrum-perforatingly. "He'll eat my chinchilla!"

desk. At least, he thought he did. But somehow, he must have missed.

Because the basket fell onto the floor with a crash, breaking the catch that held the lid shut and catapulting Sammy out into the classroom.

"Eeeeeeeeek!" screamed Chloe, eardrum-perforatingly. "He'll eat my chinchilla!"

But Sammy didn't even look at the
ball of fluff. He shot straight out of
the classroom door, down the stairs,
past the head teacher's office – knock-
ing over the nature table, scattering
fossils and interesting sorts of moss
everywhere – and out into the playground.

By the time Harry caught up with him, Sammy had joined in a game of football that the Year 6 boys were playing, and had already made two stunning saves. And, as luck would have it, that just happened to be the moment when Mr Hathaway, the teacher in charge of the school football team, came out into the playground to blow the whistle. His jaw dropped. For a moment, he stood with the whistle poised, unable to bring his lips together to blow it. Recovering himself, he blew a loud blast. The football match stopped.

"Who does that cat belong to?" bellowed Mr Hathaway.

Everyone froze. Mr Hathaway was well known for his volcano impersonations.

"Er," said Harry, nervously. "He's mine, Mr Hathaway. I'm afraid he escaped from—"

But Mr Hathaway wasn't listening to Harry's excuses. "He's playing in the match against St Botolph's tomorrow. Kick-off's at 11 a.m. Have him at the playing field by 10.45 sharp!"

Chapter Three

Sammy Makes the Difference

The next day, which was Saturday, Priory Road Primary beat St Botolph's Junior school 1–0. That may not sound too surprising, except that just the term before, St Botolph's had beaten Priory Road 22–1. (And Priory Road only got that goal because the St Botolph's team had felt sorry for their goalkeeper, standing around in the freezing cold with nothing to do, and given him a few shots to help him keep warm.)

The difference, of course, was the Tabby Blur between the posts.

At first, the St Botolph's players thought it was a joke. "A cat in goal?" their striker shouted. "I thought this was a football match, not a pet show!" But they soon stopped laughing, as Sammy pulled off save after save – diving at their feet, pawing away headers and leaping across the goal to tip their long range shots over the bar.

(In fact, the only thing he couldn't do was take his own goal kicks, so Jim took them for him.)

At half-time, with the score 0–0, the St Botolph's teacher complained. "It's not fair. You can't have a cat in goal!"

"Why not?" said Mr Hathaway. "There's nothing in the rules of football that says the players have to be human."

The St Botolph's teacher spluttered, but couldn't think of an answer. The match continued – and still St Botolph's couldn't get the ball past Sammy. In the end they got so fed up with him making save after save, that they gave up and sat down on the pitch.

Then Jim passed to Liam who passed to Danny who passed to Josh who shot . . . 1–0 to Priory Road.

Straight away, the referee blew the final whistle, and Priory Road had won their first match of the season. Of course, Sammy was a hero. But instead of joining in the celebrations, he stalked straight over to Harry, who bundled him up and took him home for a double helping of his favourite Liver 'n' Bacon KatBix.

After that, Sammy played in all Priory Road's matches. Match after match, he didn't let in a single goal. And because he was so brilliant, the team didn't need any defenders. So instead of their usual formation . . .

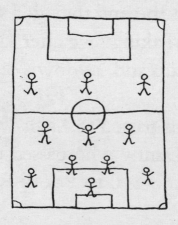

. . . they were able to play like this . . .

which meant they started to score more goals. Which meant they kept on winning. Which meant that Sammy became more and more famous.

For the second-to-last match of the season, which was the semi-final of the Hodsby and District Regional Under-11s Schools Cup, the *Hodsby Advertiser* sent a reporter and a photographer.

Of course, Priory Road won —
thanks to Sammy making super save
after super save. For the first time in
the school's history, they had reached
the Cup Final. Mr Hathaway invited
Sammy to school, where he was given
three cheers by all the children in
assembly — and a beautiful bowl for
his Liver 'n' Bacon KatBix.

Chapter Four

Sammy in the Spotlight

After that, life changed quite a bit in Harry's house. Every morning a bundle of letters would flop through the letter box, all of them addressed to Sammy. Of course, he couldn't read, so Harry had to start getting up early to open Sammy's post for him, before school.

Most of the letters were from children asking for pictures of Sammy, preferably autographed with his paw-print. But there were also lots of invitations – to open a church bazaar, take part in a sponsored Bungee Jumpathon, and present the prizes at a pub quiz night. Harry had to answer them all after he came home from school. Which didn't leave much time for his homework.

How did the Romans change Britain?
They bilt loads of roads and taught people to speak Roman.

See me about this, Harry

The phone rang all

28

the time, too – and it was nearly
always for Sammy. The *Hodsby
Advertiser* wanted to follow up their
piece on Sammy's goalkeeping
exploits with a feature on his home
life. The local radio station invited
Sammy to take part in a phone-in on
sporting facilities for Hodsby children.

And when the Liver 'n' Bacon
KatBix people, whose factory was in
Hodsby, discovered that their product
was Sammy's favourite food, they
offered him a lifetime's supply in
return for appearing in their latest TV
commercial.

The funny thing was, Sammy hardly
seemed to notice how much his life
had changed. In between his various
engagements, he just went on doing
all the usual cat stuff: sharpening his
claws on the new sofa, sleeping on the
clothes Harry's mum had just ironed,
and, of course, munching his way
through a mountain of Liver 'n'
Bacon Katbix.

But for Harry, things seemed very
different. At first, he quite enjoyed
being the owner of a local celebrity.
But quite soon, he began to feel . . .
well, a bit left out. Now that Sammy's
life was such a whirl, they never
seemed to have any time alone
together any more. Harry missed
snuggling down with Sammy on the
sofa to watch TV after school. And
staying in bed late on Saturday morning, with Sammy curled up on his
head, *purrrrrring* like a cement-mixer.

Sometimes – with so many people wanting to see Sammy, and stroke him and ask questions about how he learned to play football and when he caught his first mouse – it almost felt as if he didn't really belong to Harry any more. And that made Harry unhappy. Although, of course, he tried not to show it, because he loved Sammy, and didn't want to hurt his feelings.

Then, late one evening, when Harry had just brought Sammy home from a modelling assignment, the telephone rang. It was Gary Delve, the *Hodsby Advertiser*'s chief sports reporter.

"Sorry to call so late, Harry, but I need a quote from you on the Mudchester United story."

"The what story?" said Harry.

"Mud U," repeated Delve. "You must have heard?"

"Heard what?" said Harry.

"They're interested in that feline footballing phenomenon of yours. Bryan O'Brien is quoted as saying that he wants Sammy between the sticks at United by the start of the next season. And the rumour is, he'll be coming to watch Sammy play in the Schools Cup Final next weekend."

Bryan O'Brien was the world-famous manager of mighty Mudchester United, Premiership champions for the last three years. For a moment, Harry's mouth flapped up and down, like a goldfish. Then he recovered the power of speech. "Sammy's not going anywhere," he told the *Hodsby Advertiser*. "He's staying right here at home with me!"

Chapter Five

Sammy's Big Match Build-Up

The big match was only a few days
away now. At lunchtime on Monday,
Mr Hathaway called Harry into the
staffroom for a chat.

"So how's our Furry Friend?" he
barked.

"Oh, Sammy's fine," said Harry.

"Good," said Mr Hathaway. "I
want you to wrap him in cotton wool
between now and Saturday."

"Cotton wool?" said Harry. "I don't
think Sammy would like that."

"For goodness' sake, boy," spluttered Mr Hathaway, "I mean take

good care of him. Make sure he's eating well, and getting plenty of sleep – that kind of thing."

"Oh, I see," said Harry, wondering why Mr Hathaway couldn't just have said that, if that's what he meant.

"We don't want him injuring a paw in a catfight or pulling a hamstring falling out of a tree, just before the biggest match in Priory Road's history. I'm relying on you to make sure Sammy's one hundred per cent fit on Saturday!"

"I'll do my best," said Harry, thinking that at least it shouldn't be too
difficult to persuade Sammy to get
plenty of sleep.

After school, Harry cancelled all
Sammy's engagements for the rest of
the week. They spent the evening
together on the sofa, watching an
incredibly boring football match on
TV. *Space Geeks* was on the other
side, but Harry didn't even try to
change channel when Sammy
dropped off to sleep. He was too busy

thinking about what would happen if
Bryan O'Brien decided to sign
Sammy for Mudchester United.

At bedtime, Harry said to his mum,
"D'you think we could move to
Mudchester?"

"Mudchester?"
said his mum, who
never read the
sports pages. "Why
ever would we
want to?"

"Er, well I've heard it's very nice."

"So's Hodsby," said his mum. "And
we've lived here for years. All our
friends are here. And anyway, Dad
and I both work here."

"Couldn't you find new jobs?"

"Well, we probably could," said
Mum. "But we wouldn't want to. We
like living in Hodsby, don't we?"

"Mm," said Harry, thoughtfully.

"Well, good night, Mum."

In bed, Harry tossed and turned for
ages. If his mum and dad wouldn't
move to Mudchester, then Sammy
would have to go there by himself –
and maybe stay in a hotel, or even
live with Bryan O'Brien and his fam-
ily. Harry couldn't bear that. But, on
the other hand, he didn't want to

stand in Sammy's way. If Sammy
would be happy winning fame and
fortune as the first feline football
superstar, well, Harry would just have
to let him go . . .

Just then, the door opened a little,
and a moment later, a flying cement-
mixer landed on
Harry's head.

At least, that's what it sounded
like. No, it was no good, Harry
decided as he finally drifted off to
sleep, he couldn't part with Sammy.
He'd just have to ring up Mr
Hathaway on the morning of the Cup
Final and tell him that Sammy had
disappeared, like the time when he
got trapped in next door's dustbin for
two whole days. Of course, Mr
Hathaway would definitely go vol-
canic. But it would be worth it,
thought Harry, if it meant he didn't
have to say goodbye to Sammy.

Chapter Six

Sammy and the Mouse

The big match was about to kick off.
The final of the Hodsby and District Regional Under-11s Schools Cup was between Priory Road and – yes, you've guessed – their arch-rivals, St Botolph's. And, before you ask, here's how the teams lined up:

```
        PRIORY ROAD          ST. BOTOLPH'S
   ROWE                           DIBBLE (B)
          WILSON
                BELL    AHMED          HARRIS
          BENSON              POTTS
SAMMY   PATEL   AKUNWU  DIBBLE(A)    JOYCE   SMITH
          GIBSON               COOPER
   BROWN        COWSHILL  CROW        HAMSHERE
        SIMPSON              YAPP
```

Yes, of course, Harry had changed his mind. It wasn't because he was frightened of Mr Hathaway. At least, that wasn't the main reason. No, the main reason he couldn't go through with the Disappearing Cat plan was Jim. The day before the match, he'd come round to tea at Harry's house. But he'd been so excited about being in the Cup Final, that he hadn't been able to eat a thing – not even a Triple Chok Chok 'n' Nut Chokablok that

Harry had bought specially. That's when Harry had realized just how much winning the Cup mattered, not just to Jim, but to all his friends at Priory Road.

Which was why, at that very
moment, Sammy was bounding
around between the posts, easily
saving a few practice shots from his
teammates, as they waited for the
match to begin.

The atmosphere was electric. In the

crowd . . . well, crowd might be a bit
of an exaggeration . . . in the fairly
large group of mums and dads and a
couple of babies in buggies huddled
on the touchline, Harry searched anx-
iously for the familiar sun-tanned face

of Bryan O'Brien. There was no sign of him. Harry's hopes rose. Maybe he'd decided not to come, after all. Maybe he'd realized that a cat playing Premier League football was a ridicu-lous idea.

But then, just as the referee raised the whistle to his lips to start the match, a huge black car glided to a halt right next to the opposite touch-line. Nobody got out, but one of the smoked glass windows slid down a few inches.

Harry's heart sank. He knew at once who was inside.

The match began. At first, it was very tight. Priory Road had improved an incredible amount thanks to the confidence that having Sammy in goal gave them. But St Botolph's were determined to avenge their league defeat earlier in the season. And gradually, they started to get on top. As the match approached half-time, shot after shot rained in on the Priory Road goal – and only Sammy at his most acrobatic, leaping and pirouetting, prevented them from scoring.

The half-time whistle blew.
"They'll never get the ball past
Sammy," shouted one of the Priory
Road parents.

"That's what you think," Harry
heard the St Botolph's teacher mutter.
And he grinned in a way that made
Harry think that
maybe St Botolph's
had something up
their sleeves.

They had.

During their first
match with Priory
Road, they'd noticed something about
Sammy. They'd noticed he was a cat.
Midway through the second half, with
the score 0–0, they put their plan into
action. As their winger prepared to
take a corner, one of their strikers
went down injured in the penalty
area.

Their teacher ran onto the pitch. And while he was treating the injured player, he released from his bag . . . a large brown mouse, which started to scurry around in front of Sammy's goal. Nobody noticed. Nobody except Sammy, that is – who naturally spotted it straight away.

The winger ran up and took the corner. The ball floated high towards

Sammy's far post. What was he going to do? He had to save his team, he just had to. But he was a cat, for goodness sake, and surely no self-respecting cat could resist a really juicy mouse?

Sammy had been a cat much longer than he'd been a goalkeeper. *Whoooooshh!* he was off, after the mouse, which headed towards the changing rooms. As it disappeared

inside, a tabby blur was just inches behind. A few seconds later, Sammy emerged again, licking his lips. But, of course, by then St Botolph's had scored.

If Sammy had been anything but a cat, he would have looked ashamed of himself. But instead, he just trotted back to his goal, as if nothing had happened. Luckily, St Botolph's had only brought one mouse. And for the rest of the match Sammy played brilliantly. So brilliantly that he inspired his teammates, who started to play better than ever before. With ten minutes left, Luke's curling shot from the edge of the penalty area made the score 1–1. And then, in the dying seconds of the match, Jim leapt high above the St Botolph's defence to head in the winner.

Priory Road had won the Cup! The
players leapt up and down and hugged
each other. On the touchline, so did
their mums and dads. Sammy purred
and rubbed his head against the goal-

post. Harry was so excited that, for a moment, he'd forgotten all about Bryan O'Brien. But when he remembered and looked across to the opposite touchline, the enormous black car had disappeared . . .

Chapter 7

Sammy Settles Down

"Fair's fair, the lad Sammy played great," Bryan O'Brien told the BBC's Phil Normal on the news, later that evening. "But, at the end of the day, Phil, we've got to face it, the lad is, basically . . . a cat."

"So you won't be signing him for Mudchester United, after all?"

"No, Phil. Not after what I saw today. It wouldn't be fair to our fans. You can't have a Premier League goalkeeper who goes AWOL every time he sees a mouse. I mean, good luck to the lad, but he's just not right for Mud U . . ."

Curled up on the sofa with Sammy, Harry heaved a huge sigh of relief.

But straight away, he wished he hadn't. Maybe he was just being selfish, wanting Sammy to stay at home in Hodsby with him. Maybe he should have encouraged Sammy more. Maybe Sammy would have been happier living in Mudchester and playing in front of huge crowds every week . . .

On the sofa next to him, Sammy yawned and stretched out on his back, with his legs in the air. He didn't look too upset, thought Harry, going into the kitchen to get him an extra bowl of Liver 'n' Bacon KatBix.

And, as it turned out, Harry needn't have worried. From that day on, he noticed that Sammy seemed to be gradually losing interest in football.

He didn't trot out hopefully into the garden as soon as he'd finished his breakfast any more. He didn't gallop around madly, chasing his tail, when Jim came round for tea. He even let Harry watch *Space Geeks* without scratching him once, when he could have been watching a very exciting 0–0 draw between Spartak Lichtenstein and Sporting Arctic Circle on the other side.

At first, Harry thought that Sammy
was probably just exhausted, and that
he'd be back on top goalkeeping form
when the next football season began.
But, as the summer passed, Sammy
showed even less interest in football.
In fact, he hardly seemed to go out-

doors at all any more. Quite often, when Harry was in the garden, there was no sign of Sammy. It seemed his Tabby Blur days were behind him.

Of course, everyone wanted to know why. But Harry couldn't

explain it. He thought that perhaps chasing the St Botolph's mouse had somehow reminded Sammy that he was – as Bryan O'Brien had pointed out – basically a cat, and that cats have better things to pounce upon than a spherical lump of inflated white plastic.

Or maybe, thought Harry, as
Sammy thudded heavily into his lap
one evening, he was just getting a
little too fat for football – chomping
his way through box after box of free
Liver 'n' Bacon Katbix.

But despite these possible explana-
tions, Harry was puzzled by the furry
phenomenon's farewell to football.

Until one day, Harry discovered
that Sammy had a new hobby...

THE END